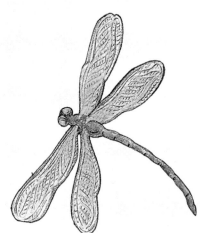

Dec. 25, 2003

to Alexia

Love, Papa

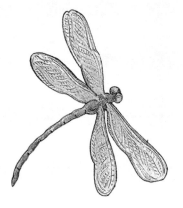

What's Inside Miss Molly's Locket?

Written by Louise Croft
and Illustrated by
Sherri Buck Baldwin

Text by Louise Croft.
Illustrations by Sherri Buck Baldwin.
© Copyright 2000
All Rights Reserved. Printed in the U.S.A.

Published by Lang Books
A Division of R.A. Lang Card Company, Ltd.
514 Wells Street • Delafield, WI 53018
262.646.2211 • www.lang.com

10 9 8 7 6 5 4 3
ISBN: 0-7412-0825-3

Presented to:

_____

From:

_____

on this date:

_____

To the most important teachers
in my life…Mom and Dad.

Louise

For Katie and Spencer,
who have taught me so much.

Sherri

Miss Molly was a teacher
at a school just down the way.
In the morning she would walk there,
each and every day.

But, just before she left her house,

her keys tucked in her pocket,
she carefully placed around her neck
a very special locket.

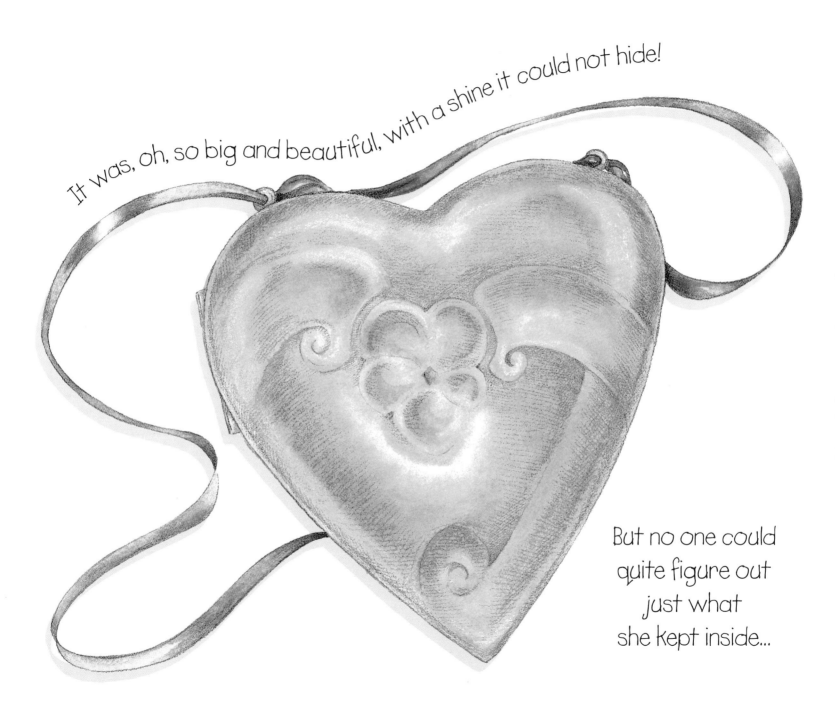

It was, oh, so big and beautiful, with a shine it could not hide!

But no one could quite figure out just what she kept inside...

The school day would begin when the loud bell rang outside.

The children would arise to pledge allegiance with *much* pride.

Teamwork

Never settle for less than your best.

Then the day was off and running –
there were many things to learn.
But wondering about that locket
made their "thinking wheels" turn.
Guessing and waiting –
they couldn't take it any longer –
the suspense inside would grow
strong, and even stronger.

Alabama Alaska

A+

Homework

Classroom Rules

Show respect

George Washington, John Adams, Thomas...

Arizona Arkansas California Colorado...

Current Events

Every syllable must have a vowel
a e i o u ... y

Have the courage to be yourself.

$\frac{1}{6} + \frac{3}{4} = \frac{2}{12} + \frac{9}{12} = \frac{11}{12}$

49×14
196
49

406×53
1218
2030

3208×9
28,871 ✓

$8\overline{)1936}$
244
16
33
32

Reduce: $\frac{15}{27}$

$$\begin{array}{r} 68 \\ \times\ 3 \\ \hline 204 \end{array} \qquad \begin{array}{r} 68 \\ \times 30 \\ \hline 2040 \end{array} \qquad \begin{array}{r} 40 \\ \times\ 5 \\ \hline 200 \end{array} \qquad \begin{array}{r} 40 \\ \times 50 \\ \hline 2000 \end{array}$$

$$\begin{array}{r} 436 \\ \times\ 4 \\ \hline \end{array} \qquad \begin{array}{r} 436 \\ \times 40 \\ \hline \end{array} \qquad \begin{array}{r} 670 \\ \times\ 8 \\ \hline \end{array} \qquad \begin{array}{r} 670 \\ \times 80 \\ \hline \end{array}$$

A hand would raise,
    and wave and wave
  frantically in the air.
Miss Molly knew what was coming
and would grin from ear to ear.

"Tell us the secret
of the locket,"
a child might
sometimes ask.

Miss Molly would refuse and say,
"Please get back on task."

The mystery grew so large—
oh, why this need to hide?
Until one day Miss Molly said,
"Something special is inside."

It was a brisk fall day –
the sun was beaming down.
The children were out for recess
and they gathered all around.

It was not time for jokes and games,
but for the children to decide...

What DID Miss Molly keep in her locket,
hidden deep inside?!

Campbell was the first to speak –
his mind was quickly ticking.
He imagined it held a lollipop
that you could never stop licking.

Kellen exclaimed, "You are wrong,"
in his all-knowing tone.
"It is her pet lizard
that she cannot leave home alone."

Caitlin thought the boys were silly
(and she, oh so smart).

She knew it had to be the man
who had stolen Miss Molly's heart.

Tommy listened to them all
and knew HIS idea to be the best—
it just had to be the answers
to every single test!

Ella disagreed—
"It is magic pixie dust!"
(Miss Molly then could put a spell
on those she did not trust).

Back inside, every child
went to take a seat.
Still confused, they hung their heads,
sad and in defeat.

A gloomy feeling filled the room,
and each child in every chair.
They each looked at Miss Molly,
faces covered with despair.

"Could someone, please, tell me
what is wrong with all of you?
There really is no need for you
to sit there looking blue."

Maya was so brave
and often spoke up for the class.
She mustered up the courage
and broke the silence at last.

"Miss Molly,
you wear your locket
every day to school,
and you know that all of us
think it's really cool.
Countless times we've begged
to know what is inside.
We are tired of not knowing...
our frustration,
we can no longer hide."

Miss Molly scratched her head
and thought for just a minute...
"Now is the time I should let
each child look in it."

Homework:
Spelling bee on Mon[day]
American History [chap]ter 3
Arithmetic - page[s]

Bur Oa[k]

Sugar Maple

"Before I share my secret
for each of you to see,
I want you to know that what is inside
is very special to me."

Then each child stood in line,
patiently in place,
and what they saw
when they looked inside...

was their own wonderful face!

For it was a mirror inside the locket that looked so smart...

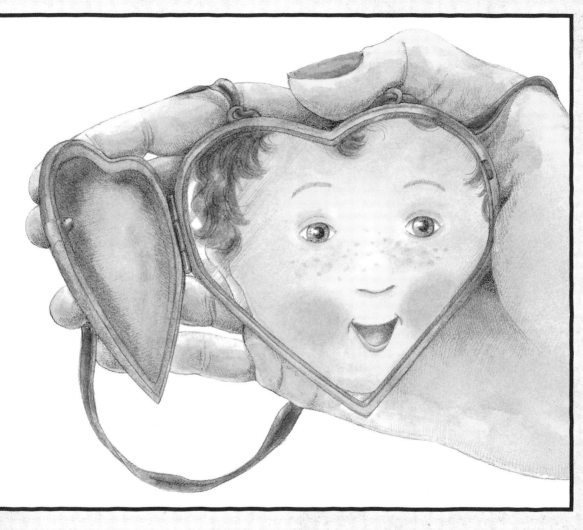

because each student Miss Molly taught...

she kept close to her heart.